Note: Hedgehogs don't live in the wild in North America, but these small mammals do live in the woods in Europe (as well as Africa and parts of Asia).

Have you ever seen a hedgehog at a zoo?
Or do you know someone who has one as a pet?
They are really cute!

Luke and Lottie

Fall Is Here!

Clavis

NEW YORK

Fall is here!
Luke and Lottie are going to play outside.
They are putting on their jackets and rubber boots.
Lottie is all ready.
"Hurry up, Luke! It'll be dark outside soon!" Lottie calls.

The wind blows the leaves from the trees.
"Look!" Lottie cries. "Luke, did you see that? There's a squirrel!"
But Luke is busy throwing leaves in the air and laughing.

"Ouch!" Luke calls. "These leaves are prickly!"

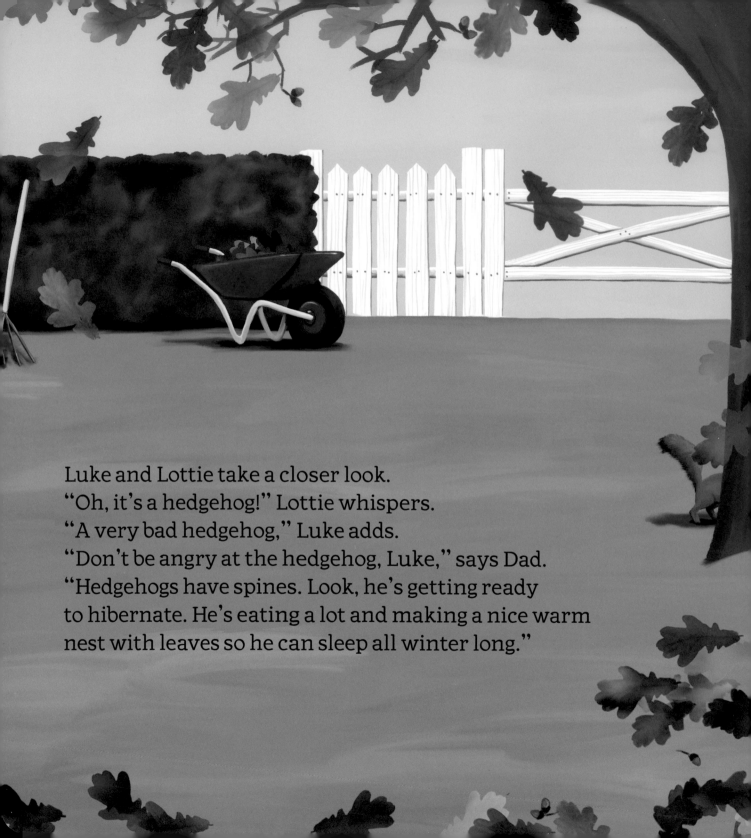

Luke and Lottie take a closer look.
"Oh, it's a hedgehog!" Lottie whispers.
"A very bad hedgehog," Luke adds.
"Don't be angry at the hedgehog, Luke," says Dad.
"Hedgehogs have spines. Look, he's getting ready
to hibernate. He's eating a lot and making a nice warm
nest with leaves so he can sleep all winter long."

Luke and Lottie want to help the hedgehog build
his nest. They put the hedgehog underneath
a bush and gather a pile of leaves.
"That's a nice home for our hedgehog," Lottie says softly.

Luke and Lottie gather nuts
and put them in their pockets.
"Does the hedgehog eat nuts, Dad?" Lottie asks.
"No, I think hedgehogs eat worms and insects," says Dad
"But maybe he would like a bowl of water."

Suddenly, it starts to rain.
Luke jumps into a puddle.
Lottie laughs and joins him.
It's fun to splash together!

It's getting dark outside. The rain is softly
tapping against the window. The hedgehog is in
his little house and Luke and Lottie are inside theirs.
Mom is bringing them hot chocolate to drink. Yum!
Luke yawns.
"Are you tired?" Mom asks.
"Yes," Luke nods. "Maybe it's time for me to start hibernating too!"